Weekly Reader Children's Book Club presents

THE AMAZING MR. PROTHERO

Also by Honor Arundel

Emma in Love
Emma's Island
The Girl in the Opposite Bed
Green Street
The High House
The Longest Weekend
The Terrible Temptation
The Two Sisters

THE AMAZING MR. PROTHERO

by
Honor Arundel

Illustrated by
Jane Paton

THOMAS NELSON INC.
Nashville / Camden / New York

No character in this story is intended to represent any actual person; all the incidents of the story are entirely fictional in nature.

 Published by Thomas Nelson Inc., Nashville, Tennessee.

Library of Congress Catalog Card Number: 70–181673
International Standard Book Number: 0–8407–6210–0
0–8407–6211–9 NLB

Printed in the United States of America

Weekly Reader Children's Book Club Edition

CONTENTS

1

Mr. Prothero Takes Steps

Julia's dog, Prothero, had chosen his own name. He was a big dog, covered with long gray and white hair that almost hid his bright dark eyes. He had black velvet flopped-over ears and a huge plumed tail that was continually knocking over ashtrays, flower vases, and milk glasses. And he liked and usually got his own way. He was supposed to sleep in his basket in the kitchen but he almost always found his way onto the living-room sofa. He was strictly forbidden to lie on beds but after his early-morning walk he would sneak upstairs for a short nap on Julia's bed, leaving large muddy pawmarks on her bedclothes.

And he liked leaning out of the window at a most alarming angle, his big back paws on the window seat and his big front paws right on the sill, barking encouragement to any of his friends in the street and sniffing the enticing smells from the restaurant across the street. Julia and her mother liked leaning out of the window, too—though not at such a dangerous angle—to watch the tourists on their way to visit Edinburgh Castle, taking photographs of the houses and each other. Once a lady tourist called out,

"Gee, isn't he cute?" and took a photograph of Prothero, and Julia was convinced that he smirked with satisfied vanity. After that he liked leaning out of the window more than ever, in spite of repeated warnings that he would fall out.

The tourists annoyed Julia's father, who preferred to read the paper. He said they made him feel like an animal at the zoo and besides, storekeepers raised prices because of them.

At first Prothero had been called Scamp. But one day about a year ago, when Julia was taking him for a run in the rough hilly part of Princes Street Gardens, where dogs are allowed to run loose, he galloped off and disappeared.

"Scamp! Sca–amp!" she called despairingly and when she had almost given him up for lost he bounded toward her, flopped down in the

grass, panting, with a huge pink wet tongue dripping moisture all around him, and said quite distinctly in a gruff voice,

"Stop calling me Scamp. My name's Mr. Prothero."

"But we've always called you Scamp," Julia replied.

"Quite. But I don't care for the name. It's undignified."

"But Mr. Prothero's too difficult," said Julia, mixing up the letters and coming out with something like "Pottlerow." "I mean, Potherlow, I mean—"

"You're hopeless. Prothero. *Mr. Prothero.*"

"Potterow," said Julia. "And why should I say Mister? You're one of the family."

"True," said Prothero condescendingly. "You can leave off the Mister."

"All right, Pothlerow."

"And if you call me Scamp again I'll know what to do," said Prothero, wrinkling back his upper lip in a sinister way and showing large white pointed teeth.

"And you'd better tell your parents too," he

added. "I'm sick of this eternal Scamp."

"I don't see what I can do," began Julia, but Prothero, springing to his feet, led the way home, flinging over his shoulder,

"Time to eat. Hurry up, pieface, I'm dying of thirst and starvation."

They set off up the hill together and Prothero bounded around like an ordinary dog, sniffing in the grass and chasing a cat that sat preening itself in the sun. He didn't speak again and Julia began to wonder if she had imagined the conversation. But you couldn't imagine a name like Prothero.

Prothero raced into the kitchen and banged his water bowl around the room as he always did when it was empty and he wanted a drink.

"Potterow's thirsty," said Julia to her mother and went to fill the bowl for him. He gulped the water down noisily and followed her into the living room, where the family always sat as the kitchen was too small for anything but cooking.

"What did you call Scamp just now?" asked her mother, who was drinking a cup of tea while she wondered what she ought to be doing instead.

Prothero looked at Julia in a meaningful way and growled softly under his breath.

"Prothero?" said Julia, getting the name right for the first time. "Oh, you mean Prothero."

"That's a queer kind of name for a dog."

"Scamp's babyish. He's a grown-up dog now," said Julia, acting under inspiration.

"Listen, Dad, to the fancy name our Julia's thought up for Scamp," said Julia's mother to Julia's father, who was sitting in his shirt sleeves by the open window reading the paper.

"What?" asked Julia's father, looking up.

"Pother something or other."

"*What?*"

"Pottlerow."

"Prothero," said Julia patiently. "Mr. Prothero."

"You can't change a dog's name," said her father. "He wouldn't answer to it."

Julia was stumped. She looked at Scamp (I mean Prothero) glaring at her from under his gray tangled hair and had another inspiration.

"Tell him," she said to her parents, "to do something, calling him Scamp. And then I will, calling him Prothero, and we'll see."

"Scamp," said her mother, "good dog, bring me my knitting bag."

Prothero growled faintly and looked bored.

"Scamp!" repeated Julia's mother. "Off you go, Scamp, my knitting bag, please Scamp."

Prothero utterly ignored her, shut his eyes, rested his nose on his front paws, and made a rude snoring noise.

"What's got into the dog!" exclaimed Julia's father. "Scamp! Here, sir, Scamp! Scamp!"

Prothero kept his eyes shut and made more snoring noises.

It was time for Julia to take over.

"Prothero, please, Mr. Prothero," she said, "come here for a minute."

Prothero opened his eyes, sprang briskly to his feet, went to Julia and looked at her questioningly.

"Prothero, would you please get Mother's knitting bag?"

With a swish of his tail that nearly swept Julia's mother's cup of tea off the table, Prothero went over to the shelves that held books, magazines, the radio, and other assorted odds and ends. He picked up the knitting bag with one stroke of his paw, gathered it gently into his mouth, and deposited it on Julia's mother's lap.

"Thank you, Scamp," she said delightedly. Prothero growled and made as if to snatch the knitting bag back again. "I mean Pro–Proddlethrow."

"Prothero, Mother."

"Prothero," said Julia's mother faintly.

Prothero licked her hand as if he were a kind teacher rewarding a favorite pupil. Then he gave Julia a wet, sloshy kiss in the middle of her face, found a nice cool patch of floor, stretched out and went to sleep.

With his change of name Prothero became more and more of a bully and though he didn't often speak to Julia, when he did, it was nearly always to insult her or to order her around.

However, whenever she was unhappy or worried he could be marvelously sympathetic. One afternoon he found her lying on her bed looking gloomy and just about to start crying. He jumped up beside her, licked around her ears with a warm, gentle tongue, then he put his cold, damp nose into her hand and snuggled up close.

"What's the matter, pieface? Tell Uncle Prothero; he'll sort out your problems and right your wrongs."

"It's Mother's birthday tomorrow. I've just remembered."

"Nothing wrong with a birthday. Cake. Delicious! Probably a chocolate or two."

"But I haven't bought her a present. And I've only got nine pence."

"Nine pence. Hmmm. Never mind. Leave it to Prothero, Prothero the ingenious, Prothero the brave." He jumped off the bed and shook himself. Then, apparently deciding that Julia had had enough sympathy for one day, he started to order her around as usual.

"Hurry up. Brush your hair. Go and get your leash."

"It's your leash, not mine," protested Julia, but she slid obediently off the bed.

"Nonsense. It's you that needs a leash—to stop you from getting run over."

"But I don't wear a collar."

"Whose fault's that?" demanded Prothero rudely.

It was true that Prothero did guide Julia through traffic—he was very reliable in some ways—but he always behaved as if he were leading her instead of the other way around, which was insulting to Julia's pride.

"Perhaps I could buy her a cake of soap, the nice pink smelly kind," began Julia, following Prothero out into the street.

"Soap? Ugh! Horrible stuff. Reminds people of baths. No, we'll find something better than that. Now hurry up, pieface."

He dragged Julia across the street, threading his way expertly between two buses and a furniture truck.

"We'll never find anything nice for nine pence."

"Nonsense and balderdash. We shall Take Steps."

Prothero had obviously misunderstood the expression "Take Steps." He took it literally, because there were a great many steps leading downhill from Julia's part of Edinburgh. The steps he meant this time led down from a sort of hole in the street into a dark tunnel and then, surprisingly, out into Victoria Street, where there were many interesting shops. First there was a window full of prints of old Edinburgh, showing curly trees and unfamiliar houses and people in funny old-fashioned clothes.

"Here we are," said Prothero importantly. "Get her a picture to hang on the wall. Go in and ask the price."

Julia hated going into shops by herself. It made her feel shy, and when she felt shy she nearly always stammered. But Prothero dragged her in by force. There was simply no way of avoiding the tall, dignified owner, who looked at them as if they had no right to come into his shop at all.

"H-how m-much are the p-p-pictures?" stammered Julia.

"Various prices," said the man in a bored voice. "Anything from fifty pence to five pounds."

"Th-thank you," mumbled Julia and escaped as fast as possible.

Then there was a shop that sold wooden things, bowls and egg cups and spoons and three-legged stools and broom handles.

"What about an egg cup?" said Prothero. "Always useful. I like a boiled egg for breakfast myself. Go in and ask how much they are."

"They're marked," said Julia with a sigh of relief. "Twenty pence."

Then came a window entirely devoted to string and rope in huge bales.

"I could buy Mother some string; she's always short of string," suggested Julia.

"Rotten idea. Who wants string?" snapped Prothero, dragging her along. "We'll go to the junk shops. We'll find a good bargain for nine pence in a junk shop."

The Grassmarket, a street at the bottom of the steep curving street, was full of antique stores and junk shops. Some were very elegant with just a little shiny wooden chest or table placed in the center of the window. Others were shabbier, and tightly packed with plates and jugs and broken-down shoes and teaspoons.

Prothero was very impressed with a big gilt birdcage but Julia knew it would cost more than nine pence, and in any case, they didn't have a bird.

"You're just too scared to go in and ask," said Prothero nastily. "Now here's a likely shop. Go in and dig around."

While Julia was trying to get up enough courage to do this, Prothero noticed two dogs playing in the street. He could never resist insulting other dogs, any more than he could resist chasing cats. One dog was smooth-coated, black and white, with a black patch over one eye that made it look like a pirate. The other was reddish, with a lively face and a tail wound up tight like a corkscrew.

"Rogues and vagabonds," said Prothero, scornfully. "Scavengers, garbage-pail robbers, delinquents."

"Come on, Prothero," pleaded Julia, trying to pull him along.

"Slobs, yobs, greasers, gutter dogs," said Prothero in a louder voice, and the dogs looked

up and replied with what sounded like equal insults—though Julia couldn't understand them.

"Who—never—has—a—bath, who—never—has—a—bath, who—never—washes—his—feet," rumbled Prothero. He took a few steps toward the dogs, then stopped, his tail swishing angrily, his head cocked in a threatening way.

The two dogs growled in return. Their fur stood up around their necks. Their tails lashed, too.

"Come on, Prothero," begged Julia. "Oh, please come on. *Please* be a good dog."

"Come on and get it," sneered Prothero. "I'm not afraid of rogues and vagabonds. I'll show them."

He jerked the leash out of Julia's hands and stalked, bent-legged, toward the two dogs, jeering and showing his teeth. The next minute they were all mixed up together, snapping, snarling, biting, rolling over and over.

"Prothero!" shrieked Julia. She looked around for help. She was standing outside a very junky junk shop, and no owner was in sight. It

soon became clear that she would either have to open the door and go in without the moral support of Prothero, or go home alone, leaving Prothero to his fate. It was not an easy decision to make. She looked back at the dogs, then at the shop, and then back at the dogs again. Two against one! She would simply *have* to rescue Prothero, she decided. So she bravely opened the door and went in. At the back of the shop a dark, squat, but kind-looking man sat writing something at a desk which was covered with dust and dirty teacups and objects of all kinds.

"P-p-please," Julia stammered, "p-please could you h-help me? My d-d-d-dog . . ."

The man looked up.

"What?" he said. But he rose to his feet and came over to Julia in a friendly way.

"You're upset. What's the matter?"

"My d-d-d-dog!" gasped Julia.

The man strode into the street and grasped the situation at once. He pulled Prothero out of the squalling muddle of dogs, separated the other two with a couple of well-aimed kicks, and sent them racing fearfully away.

"Let me get at them," growled Prothero, jerking at his leash. "I'll show them. I'll tear them to ribbons."

"Behave," said the junk-shop owner severely. Prothero behaved. His anger suddenly left him and he gave Julia an apologetic look.

"I'm sorry," he muttered, "lost my temper. But you should have heard what they called me. And you. I don't allow persons under my escort to be insulted."

"Come inside a minute," said the junk-shop owner to Julia. "You look all shaken up."

"I'm all right," said Julia.

"Out for a walk?"

"I was looking for a birthday present," explained Julia, her stammer forgotten. "I thought I might find something."

"Look around, my girl, look around. Who's the present for?"

"My mother. It's her birthday tomorrow."

"Would she like a plate?"

"I've only got nine pence," said Julia, feeling she ought to make this clear immediately.

"There's a pile there priced at ten pence. But I might make a special reduction in your case."

There were coal scuttles and paraffin lamps, bedroom jugs and glass decanters, cutlery, kettles, and strings of beads. Julia carefully threaded her way through them, pulling along a panting and (she hoped) repentant Prothero, and started examining the plates. Some were broken, some were cracked, all were dirty, and her heart sank. Mum wouldn't possibly like a dirty old plate.

"Let's get out of this," mumbled Prothero.

Julia lifted her hand as if to smack him. For once he could just do what he was told. After all, she had been brave enough to go into the shop by herself in order to rescue him. She went on looking at the plates until she found one she liked. It was the sort of white that is almost pale blue, with a rich border of darker blue and gold and a little blue butterfly in the center. She rubbed a little of it clean and looked at it again. Prothero perked up and forgot he was in disgrace.

"That's nice," he said. "It would do for my dinner, but the edges aren't high enough. I like a good high edge. Something to work my tongue against."

"I like this one," Julia said hesitantly to the junk-shop owner.

"A beautiful plate. If I had a set of these I'd make my fortune."

He took the plate, rubbed it with his sleeve, and held it up to the light with a satisfied smile.

"Yes, I'd make my fortune with a set of these. But you can have it for nine-pence, my girl."

Julia felt in her pocket and handed over the money.

"Thank you," she said. "Th-thank you."

"Any time," said the junk-shop owner. He opened the door for her politely and showed her out.

Holding the plate carefully in one hand and Prothero's leash in the other, Julia walked slowly up the street toward home. Prothero had recovered his high spirits. He waved his tail gaily and began boasting.

"I told you we'd find something nice. Ideal present. Just what the doctor ordered. Wouldn't mind a plate like that myself. Except, of course, for the edges."

"You're a horrible dog," said Julia, "you disgraced me. Fighting in the street. You know you're not supposed to. If I told my dad he'd beat you."

"All's well that ends well," said Prothero jauntily. "If I hadn't been in a fight you wouldn't have dared to go into the shop. I know *you*. And if the man hadn't been sorry for you he wouldn't have offered you the plate for ninepence. See? I told you you'd find a bargain if you took my advice."

His conceit was unbearable.

"If I hadn't rescued you, you might have been killed," Julia retorted.

Prothero didn't reply.

"Come on, pieface, and watch the traffic," he said coldly, a few moments later.

Julia washed the plate and dried it until all the colors shone. She wrapped it in tissue paper and put it on the breakfast table next morning and her mother unwrapped it with exclamations of surprise and delight.

"What a lovely plate! Look, Dad, what our Julia's found. I'll put it in the display cabinet and we'll only use it if we have guests. How in the world did you find it, love? It's the nicest plate I ever had."

Julia purred and then she was conscious of Prothero at her side, showing his teeth and making believe to nip her ankle.

"Prothero helped me," she said quickly.

Prothero smirked and accepted the top of Julia's boiled egg held out to him in a teaspoon. Then he slipped unobtrusively from the room, no doubt to find if Julia's bedroom door was open so that he could have a snooze on her bed.

2

Mr. Prothero Fights a Battle

"I think it's time you managed to come home from school by yourself," Julia's father said to her one day at breakfast.

"Do you think you can manage, dear?" asked her mother anxiously.

"Of course I can," Julia said indignantly.

"We're going to have a new baby," her father went on, "and I want your mother to have as much rest as possible."

Julia was terribly excited.

"We're going to have a new baby," she told

Prothero, who always took her to the bus stop in the morning before trotting off to pick up the daily paper.

"A new baby? What for?"

"You and I will be able to look after it together," said Julia happily.

"Hm," snorted Prothero, "I've got my hands full enough with you."

The thought of coming home alone didn't alarm Julia in the least because there was a kind traffic guard who stopped the cars and trucks to let the children cross the road to the bus stop.

At first she hadn't liked school at all. She felt shy with the other girls and when teachers pounced on her and asked her questions, even simple things like what was her name and had she any brothers or sisters, she found herself stammering and this made some of the children call her "Jujujulia." And the boys made her feel particularly nervous. They always seemed to be fighting, rolling over in the playground, bashing each other with their school bags, pretending to machine-gun each other, uttering strange yells and whistles and insults at the girls. Thank goodness they had their own playground!

Julia didn't complain to her parents because she felt rather ashamed of being shy and stammering. But she told Prothero, who was entirely sympathetic.

"School," he sneered, "lot of nonsense. Nonsense and balderdash. I never went to school and look at me."

"But Prothero, you're a dog," explained Julia.

"So what?"

"I have to learn how to read and write and do arithmetic," explained Julia, "and pass exams and so on, otherwise I'll never be properly grown up."

"Never passed an exam in my life and I'm grown up," said Prothero.

"I've told you, it's different for dogs," Julia repeated.

"I can take you across the road and stop you getting run over and pick up the paper and look after the house and answer the door and protect you all from burglars—and *I* never went to school," said Prothero, who had a high opinion of himself.

"Well, I've got to go," said Julia gloomily, "for years and years and years."

"Thank goodness I'm a dog," retorted Prothero.

After a while, of course, Julia did settle down and begin to enjoy her new life as a schoolgirl. It made her feel grown up to wear a white shirt with a tie and a navy-blue jacket with the school badge on the pocket and carry a school bag strapped to her back.

But she still hated boys and kept out of their way as far as possible. There was one gang who were particularly unpleasant. They all had bare scrubbed scarred knees and identical lively freckled faces. The only difference was in the colors of their hair. One was red, one very dark, and two were brown. Now that she went home alone, they began following Julia to the bus stop, making remarks which she knew were impolite even though she couldn't understand them properly.

One day Julia was a little late in leaving school, as she had lost one of her gloves and had to get it back from the janitor. She hoped the boys would have all gone home and was dismayed to find them still lying in wait for her. They surrounded her and danced around and around her until she felt dizzy, pulling her school bag and bumping into her with exaggerated "Oh, excuse me's" and "Sorry's."

Julia pretended not to see or hear them but it became more and more difficult.

At last one boy, braver than the rest, snatched Julia's school bag and the books spilled onto the sidewalk. This was really too much and Julia started to run after him, but she tripped over the bag and fell down. Although falling on her knee on the hard pavement brought tears to her eyes, she determined not to cry and bent down to pick up her books so that no one could see her face.

"You ought to be ashamed of yourselves, teasing a little girl," said a man waiting at the bus stop, advancing on the boys, who galloped off. He helped Julia to pick up her books, patted her on the shoulder, and rubbed her knee with his handkerchief.

"Are you all right now?" he asked kindly.

"Yes, th-thanks," said Julia.

Then the bus came.

Julia wanted to hurry home and tell her

mother, but she knew that if she did her mother would insist upon meeting her every day, and that would be too babyish for words.

Prothero just happened to be passing the bus stop when Julia got off the bus and he noticed immediately that something was wrong.

"What's the matter, pieface?"

"Boys," said Julia.

"Rough, are they?"

"They're horrible," burst out Julia.

"What did they do?"

"They teased me and upset my school bag."

"Rogues and vagabonds," said Prothero indignantly. "I may not have passed any exams, but I could teach them a thing or two. What's more, I shall. I know how to deal with boys, Prothero the ingenious, Prothero the brave."

He led the way home, tail flying, head in the air.

"What do you mean, deal with them, Prothero?" asked Julia, running to catch up with him.

"Wait and see, pieface," said Prothero, but he stuck his cold nose into her hand and gave her an affectionate lick. Julia felt comforted.

That night when she had gone to bed Prothero came upstairs and scratched at the door. Julia let him in and he jumped up onto the bed beside her.

"Listen," he said, "I've got a plan. All carefully worked out."

"Oh, good, Prothero."

"When do they bother you, the boys, I mean?"

"When I wait for the bus."

"What time?"

"Half past three. But Prothero, you can't tell time," Julia protested.

"I have my methods," said Prothero haughtily.

"And you don't know where the school is."

Prothero snorted impatiently.

"As if a little thing like that could stump me," he said. "Now don't you worry. Leave it all to Uncle Prothero. I shall Take Steps. And remember, you are not to recognize me, under any circumstances. It's part of the plan."

"All right," said Julia, "but I wish you would tell me what the plan is."

"Wait and see," said Prothero. "Now I think I shall sleep here tonight." And he arranged himself snugly in the very center of the bed, nose to tail, like a round, furry, and extremely heavy cushion.

Julia was left with a very small portion of

bed. She tried to straighten her legs, but Prothero was too heavy.

"Now Prothero, you know you're not allowed," she began.

"Lie still," he grunted. "Stop chattering and don't snore."

Julia felt more cheerful at school the next day. She read a whole page in her reader without a mistake and the picture she painted was hung up on the wall. And she was actually looking forward to the bell ringing at half past three to find out about Prothero's plan.

But when she came out of school there wasn't a sign of him. The man stopped the traffic to let her cross the street and the four boys followed close behind, nudging each other and giggling. Julia's cheerfulness disappeared. How could she have imagined that even a clever dog like Prothero could know when it was half past three and find his way to a strange part of Edinburgh? He had just been boasting as usual. She decided she would have to deal with the boys herself, so when they began jostling her, she said in a voice meant to sound angry but which actually just sounded frightened:

"Leave me alone."

"Leave me alone, leave me alone," mimicked the boys.

They formed a ring around her and started singing in fierce high-pitched voices:

"Ring-around-a-rosy, ring-around-a-rosy."

"Stop it," squeaked Julia, who knew quite well that when it came to "All fall down," someone would accidentally-on-purpose bump into her and she would be the one to fall.

At that precise moment something large and gray and furry bounded in among them, knocking down one boy and scattering the others. It was Prothero. A strange, wild, savage Prothero, with bared teeth and eyes glittering behind the hair that drooped over them.

Just in time Julia remember that she had promised not to recognize him. She stood and watched excitedly while Prothero bent growling over the sprawling boy, and the other boys watched too.

"Run for it, Pete," they called. "Hit him one and run for it."

"Pull him off," yelped the fallen boy, "he's biting me."

Prothero was certainly going through the motions of biting him and for a moment Julia was alarmed. Dogs were not allowed to bite, she knew, and if they did the police came and

BUS STOP

took them away. Perhaps Prothero had lost his temper and forgotten this. He sounded terribly fierce.

Julia ran forward quickly and seized him by the collar and pulled him backward, still snarling and struggling, but when he turned his head around to look at her he gave her a definite wink. He was just play-acting after all.

The boy scrambled to his feet and looked at Julia in amazement and then rejoined his chums.

"Fat lot of use you are," he said, "leaving it all to a girl."

"Bad dog," Julia said firmly to Prothero, pretending to shake him. "Now go home. Bad dog. Go home!"

Prothero gave her another wink and streaked off up the street with his tail flying out behind him.

The boys looked sheepishly at Julia and melted away. Julia, her head held high, walked proudly to the bus stop and joined the line of waiting people.

Prothero was waiting for her when she got

off the bus, even more boastful and exuberant than usual.

"I told you I'd fix them," he said, jumping up and leaving muddy pawmarks on Julia's clean school skirt. "Prothero the brave, Prothero the avenger."

Julia hugged him. For once she felt he was not exaggerating.

"But you didn't really bite him, did you?" she asked.

"Bite him? Ugh! I wouldn't dirty my teeth on a boy like that."

"I thought you might have forgotten—that's why I pulled you off."

"It was all part of my plan, stupid," said Prothero.

"Will you come again tomorrow?"

"If you think I've nothing better to do with my time," began Prothero. "Anyhow it won't be necessary. Now what about a reward? There's the butcher's."

"Oh no, Prothero."

"Oh yes," said Prothero, leading the way.

He knew perfectly well that Julia hated going

into shops by herself, but she could hardly refuse on this occasion. Prothero did deserve a reward.

Julia particularly disliked the butcher's shop with all that red meat lying around and the carcasses of sheep hanging up with their heads still on and the butchers themselves with their long sharp knives and their bloodstained aprons. However, she gritted her teeth and went boldly inside.

"P-p-please could I have a b-b-bone," she said.

"Bone for the young lady, Jim," said the fat, cheerful butcher to his assistant.

"Bone for the young lady?" kidded the assistant.

"She says she wants a bone, Jim. The things young ladies want these days."

Julia blushed.

"It's not for me, it's for my d-dog," she mumbled.

Jim dug around in the back of the shop and handed over a big knucklebone, Prothero's fa-

vorite kind. But it might be expensive and Julia had only two pence.

"How m-much does it cost?" she asked nervously.

"For a handsome dog like this," said the butcher, coming around outside the counter and looking at Prothero, "nothing."

Prothero wagged his tail. He always appreciated compliments.

"Will he sit up for it?" the butcher asked Julia.

"No-no," said Julia hastily. Prothero stopped wagging his tail and looked sour. He regarded begging as thoroughly undignified and had firmly refused to learn.

"Cut the cackle and hand over the bone," he muttered, but luckily only Julia understood him.

"There you are, boy," said the butcher, and Prothero took the big bone in his mouth so that it stuck out on either side and walked proudly from the shop with Julia, spluttering thank-you's, following.

"Ee – ed – I – oz – hahum," Prothero said through the bone, meaning, Julia imagined, "He said I was handsome."

"You need a bath," she said severely. Prothero growled through his bone.

The next day at school Julia found to her surprise that she had become a heroine. At recess she kept seeing that she was being pointed out and there were little murmurs of "That's the girl . . . Julia something or other her name is . . . a dead-fierce dog . . . didn't turn a hair . . . just pulled it off Pete . . . Pete was dead scared . . . imagine, a girl . . . she's only little . . ." and other gratifying remarks. The news spread from the boys' to the girls' playground and several girls asked Julia exactly what had happened. "Gosh!" they kept saying, "Golly!" and "How in the world did you have the nerve?"

"It was nothing," said Julia modestly. She felt several inches taller and as if she would never be afraid again.

The four boys followed her to the bus stop as usual, but this time at a respectful distance, and she heard the boy called Pete, the dark-haired one, say in an admiring voice, "She's really tough," and then after a whispered conversation with his friends in which Julia caught the words "Go on, I dare you," he called out,

"Hey, you, Julia!"

"What?" She turned around.

"Have a piece of candy?" He held out a crumpled paper bag.

Julia took one.

"Thanks," she said coolly.

Then the boys became convulsed with giggles. They struggled and squirmed together and ran off whooping down the street.

"They say I'm really tough," Julia reported proudly to Prothero when she got home.

"I told you so. That was my plan. Mr. Prothero's master plan. Now, go and get your leash, pieface. I want to go for a walk."

"But I'm tired," objected Julia.

"Nonsense and balderdash. I've been cooped up all day and I need to stretch my legs."

"But I don't."

"Do as you're told," snapped Prothero. "We'll go into Princes Street Gardens. And bring your ball. We'll have a game."

Julia sighed. A bone yesterday. A walk and a game of ball today. That was the penalty of being in Prothero's debt.

"But I'm tough," she said to herself happily, "I'm really tough."

3

Mr. Prothero and the New Baby

Julia and her mother and father were all delighted with the new baby. His name was Roddy and he had a mass of dark hair and dark-blue eyes which he hardly ever opened because most of the time he was asleep.

But Prothero was disgusted.

When Julia's mother brought Roddy home from the hospital, he peered at the small pink object from under his gray tangled hair, sniffed the tiny clenched hand, and growled.

"Prothero!" said Julia's mother, horrified.

"Prothero!" said Julia's father, raising a hand ready to hit him.

Prothero slunk under the sofa and sulked. He didn't speak for days and when he did, it was fortunate that only Julia understood him because what he had to say was hardly polite.

"What's it for?" he sneered. "What's it do?"

"It's 'he,' not 'it,' " said Julia, rather confused.

"It looks like an 'it' to me."

"It, I mean he, will grow up into a boy," explained Julia.

"I thought you didn't like boys," said Prothero unfairly.

"Some of them are nice," said Julia. "Roddy will be. We'll bring him up properly."

"Count me out," said Prothero bad-temperedly.

Now the whole household revolved around Roddy. Julia hurried home from school and instead of taking Prothero for a run or a game of ball in Princes Street Gardens, she wheeled Roddy out in his carriage, very carefully and proudly. Prothero refused to come too. He said it was undignified for a dog of his mature years to go for a walk with a baby in a carriage. But what he really didn't like was the way people were always peering into the carriage to say, "What a beautiful baby," when they should have been saying, "What a handsome dog."

And Julia's father hurried home from work, too, so that he would be in time to watch Roddy being bathed and put to bed.

"How's the little fellow?" he would ask, picking Roddy up and holding him and talking to him instead of stroking Prothero and asking him how *he* was or pretending to wrestle with him.

And Julia's mother was always too busy washing or ironing or cuddling the baby to pay much attention to Prothero.

Prothero expressed his displeasure in several ways. He still took Julia across the street to her bus stop when she went to school but he did so rudely and gracelessly, saying, "Hurry up, pie-face, you'll be late again," or "Look where you're going, stupid."

He stopped picking up the morning paper and simply disappeared for whole days at a time on mysterious private business, usually returning messy and muddy. Indoors he was equally unpleasant. If he was inside a room he scratched to be let out, and if he was outside he scratched to be let in, and he spent a lot of time under the sofa, glaring balefully and making rude remarks under his breath. And he barked noisily at imaginary sounds when Roddy was asleep.

"When's it going to walk and talk? When's it going to learn to feed itself? When's it going to be house trained?" he demanded impatiently.

"Not for ages yet," said Julia. "But can't you see, Prothero? It's nice now—I mean, *he's* nice now. He's cuddly and sweet and he smiled at me this morning."

"Pah," snorted Prothero. "I learned all those things in a couple of weeks when I was a puppy. It's been here for months now and it hasn't improved at all."

"How many times do I have to tell you," said Julia, "it's he, not it. How would you like it if we called you 'it'?"

"I'm Mr. Prothero; everyone knows that."

But the crowning insult to Prothero's dignity came when Julia's mother said that he must have a bath because he was dirty and smelly and it was unhygienic for a dirty smelly dog to share a house with a baby.

"Come on, my boy," said Julia's father. "Bath."

Prothero was furious and galloped upstairs and hid under Julia's bed, growling, and when Julia pulled him out he spluttered,

"Dirty? Me? Nonsense and balderdash. Wash every day. Most particular. What's more, I do it myself. Don't have to be bathed like some creatures I could mention."

"Come on, Prothero," coaxed Julia. "I'll take you for a run afterward."

Julia's father had armed himself with a big towel and a cake of red carbolic soap. He ran the bath half full of warm water and plunked Prothero in the middle of it, while Julia stood beside him ready to help. Prothero struggled and shouted but Julia's father held him firmly while Julia soaped him all over, his face and his hair and his black velvet ears and his white shirt front and his long fluffy trousers and his large plumed tail. Although he was a big dog he began to look quite tiny now that he was wet all over.

"Help! help!" he shrieked. "I'm drowning. The water's too hot. The water's too cold. The

soap went in my eye. Let me out! Let me out!"

Julia pulled the plug and waited for the dirty water to drain away and then she ran in some clear water to rinse him.

"I'll die of cold. I'll get pneumonia. Help! Let me out!" yelled Prothero.

"Be quiet, you stupid animal," said Julia's father.

He lifted Prothero out and he and Julia held him still and rubbed and rubbed until they thought all the surplus water had been dried

away, but when Prothero escaped and began shaking himself they realized that they hadn't been successful. Water simply flew out of him, drenching them both.

"Grr, grr, horrible, wet, cold, beastly, hate the whole bunch of you," spluttered Prothero, running wildly around the house.

That evening Julia's mother and father had a serious conversation about whether they wouldn't have to send him away somewhere. It wasn't safe, they said, to have a bad-tempered dog in the same house with a baby.

"Oh no," groaned Julia in dismay. Of course she didn't love Prothero as much as her mother and father and Roddy, but still he was one of the family and she couldn't imagine life without him.

"He'll have to improve his behavior if he wants to stay," said Julia's father.

But Prothero's behavior didn't improve. And the climax came when he sneaked up while Julia's mother was giving Roddy his cereal and scooped up a big dollop with his tongue, so that

Julia's mother had to go and make some more.

"You're a bad dog," said Julia.

"We'll have to get rid of him," said Julia's mother.

"We'll put an advertisement in the paper: 'Home needed for badly trained, bad-mannered, bad-tempered dog,' and see who'll take you over," said Julia's father.

Prothero growled.

"They should send *it* away, not me. After all I was here first," he grumbled to Julia when they were alone in the kitchen.

"Don't be stupid!" said Julia. She was in despair. She couldn't bear the thought of Prothero being sent away. When she went to bed that night she lay awake and thought and thought of how to make Prothero behave. And at last she had an idea. Perhaps she had made a mistake by making too much of a fuss over Roddy and not nearly enough of a fuss over Prothero. She decided to change her tactics.

To begin with, Julia got a bone for him from the butcher. She and the butcher were now old friends and he teased her while he found a big bone for Prothero and she laughed and teased him back instead of blushing and stammering.

She brought the bone home and presented it to Prothero.

"What's that for?" he asked suspiciously.

"You," said Julia.

"I'm not hungry," said Prothero and shut his eyes, but when Julia went out of the room he swooped on the bone and took it under the sofa with him. It kept him quiet for the rest of the day.

The next day was Sunday and after dinner

both Julia's mother and father were sleepy and said,

"You take Roddy out for a walk, will you, dear?"

"Oh, *must* I?" said Julia with an exaggerated wail in her voice.

"You know you like taking out your little brother," said her mother in a surprised voice.

"I'm tired of taking him out. The carriage is so heavy and I can't go anywhere interesting. Anyhow I want to go out with Prothero and then we can run and play games."

Her father and mother were astonished. They didn't realize it was all part of a cunning plan.

Prothero, who was under the sofa as usual, opened an eye and quickly shut it again.

"You can have money for ice cream," said her father, leaning back in his chair and closing his eyes. He was always sleepy after Sunday dinner.

"Oh, all right," grumbled Julia, "but I'm sick of being a nursemaid."

Roddy was now eight months old. His hair

had grown thicker and darker, his eyes bluer and brighter, and his face pinker and rounder. Julia carried him downstairs very carefully and put him in his carriage, strapping him in and giving him his yellow teddy bear to hold.

Prothero appeared from nowhere.

"Might as well come too," he murmured casually. "Brought your leash. Can't be too careful. The traffic nowadays is abominable."

Julia smiled to herself. Perhaps the plan was already beginning to work!

"Babies are a nuisance," she said insincerely, stooping to kiss Roddy on his firm pink cheek, just in case he could understand and think she meant it.

"Still, we've got to do our duty," said Prothero.

Julia fastened Prothero's leash and they all walked sedately down the road and into Princes Street Gardens. It was pleasant in the gardens. The sun shone, making speckly shadows through the leaves of the trees onto the newly cut grass. There were boys playing ball, old ladies sitting on seats, bigger boys and girls lying in the sun, toddlers running and falling down and being picked up and falling down again. She could hear birds singing, the purr of a lawnmower, and the hum of the traffic in Princes Street.

Then Julia got tired. The carriage with Roddy in it *was* heavy. The sun was hot.

"Let's sit down a minute," she said to Prothero, who immediately flopped into the grass, panting. Julia put the brake on and sat down beside him. Roddy leaned back and went to sleep.

But as well as being hot and tired, Julia was thirsty, and she suddenly remembered the money her father had given her. There would be ice cream at the bottom of the hill, but the thought of wheeling the carriage down and back again was exhausting. On the other hand, Julia knew that to run down by herself would only take a minute and Roddy was safely asleep.

"Prothero," she said, "would you keep an eye on Roddy while I go for ice cream? Please, Prothero."